PLATFORM PAPERS

**QUARTERLY ESSAYS ON THE PERFORMING ARTS
FROM CURRENCY HOUSE**

||||||||||||||||||||||||||||||||||||||||||||||||||||||||||||||||

**No. 62
February 2020**

CURRENCY HOUSE

Platform Papers Partners

Platform Papers
Readers' Forum

Readers' responses to our previous essays are posted on our website. Contributions to the conversation (250 to 2000 words) may be emailed to info@currencyhouse. org.au. The Editor welcomes opinion and criticism in the interest of healthy debate but reserves the right to monitor where necessary.

Platform Papers, quarterly essays on the performing arts, is published every February, May, August and November and is available through bookshops, by subscription and on line in paper or electronic version. For details see our website at www.currencyhouse.org.au.

Performing arts markets and their conundrums

JUSTIN MACDONNELL

ABOUT THE AUTHOR

Justin Macdonnell has been employed in arts management, producing and consultancy for over forty years. His early career was occupied variously as General Manager of the State Opera of Australia, Director of the National Opera of New Zealand, Program Director of the Festival of Sydney, Executive Director of the Confederation of Australian Professional Performing Arts and Artistic Director of the Center for the Performing Arts in Miami, USA.

As principal of Macdonnell Promotions he was for twenty years one of Australia's leading arts management consultants to both the public and private sectors and to scores of arts organisations here and abroad. From 1992, through the Australia-Latin America Foundation, he ran a broad cultural exchange network between Australia and that region, managing over a hundred tours and exhibitions in that time. In those capacities he has been a veteran participant in performing arts markets on six continents.

For the past ten years he has been Executive Director of the cultural industries think tank and consulting agency, Anzarts Institute, which over the last four years has undertaken studies for Arts NSW, Art Tasmania, Arts NT, the cities of Darwin, Kununurra, the Gold

Coast, Willoughby and Marrickville; the Australia Council, Creative New Zealand, Melbourne University, SAE/Navitas, NIDA; and acted as strategic consultant for companies such as ARUP International, Brisbane Powerhouse, Sydney Dance Company, Century Venues Pty Ltd, Sydney Fringe, Riverside Theatres, Black Swan State Theatre Companym QTC, Orana Arts, Kultour, NAISDA dance college, Blackfella Films and Gadigal Broadcasting—Koori Radio.

Introduction

The performing arts market has come to occupy a central place in the cycle of transactions in live theatre, music and dance around the world. Once, the idea of the arts participating in what are undeniably trade fairs, complete with product booths, giveaways and funny hats, would have been anathema. Gradually, they have become the norm for almost any company or even individual artist wanting to secure a place on the international scene.

I came across the activity in the mid-1980s when Australian artists started to be aware of more strategic approaches to taking their work abroad than leaving it merely to chance. The Department of Foreign Affairs had opened some doors over the preceding decades, mostly in Asia, mostly in music, though the famed Marionette Theatre of Australia had also done the rounds.

The Australia Council for the Arts was largely uninterested in performing arts export. The Australian Ballet had gone on mammoth excursions heavily under-written by government. The emergent Sydney Dance Company and Circus Oz had made some inroads. A few of us discovered the North American markets and started to turn up as a little band of Aussies. We booked stands, stuck together, promoted each other's wares, watched each other's backs, made our presence felt, met some presenters and sold some shows. After a while, the Australia Council took notice and started to give us a few bob to help rent the space, cover our registrations and pay hotel nights. Sometimes the local Consul-General would throw a drinks party.

Meanwhile, Marguerite Pepper and I had created ExportOz Ltd as an umbrella to sell our mix of clients in dance, physical theatre, street theatre, contemporary music and comedy. One year, we came back and said to the Australia Council: we should do one of these markets ourselves. But where and when? Robyn Archer was about to direct the first National Festival of Australian Theatre in Canberra. That seemed a likely place to start. She joined her powerful voice to our chorus. The Performing Arts Board, as it then was, coughed up some funds. The Canberra Theatre Centre gave the space and in 1994 we were off and running. That was the Australian Performing Arts Market (APAM). About twenty international delegates came that first year. We felt we had really broken through.

Of course, there are many kinds of markets and companion events which, while they are not designated markets as such, function effectively as sites where productions are seen and traded. The more formal version ranges from the huge and grotesque such as New York's Association of Performing Arts Presenters (APAP)[1] to the less daunting of their ilk—like *Conference Internationale des Arts de la Scène* (CINARS) in Canada[2] or the Australian Performing Arts Market (APAM) here.[3] The phenomenon arose in the US where they are called for what they are: 'booking conferences,' and while today most include other activities, they are still essentially about producers securing dates for a tour. Delegates attend as an investment in that possibility.

From the US the concept, now over sixty years old, spread around the globe. There are markets in Asia, North and South America, Africa and the Pacific. Once, those of us who have been forced to become habitués used to carry to them suitcases of promotional material. Now we have a handful of USBs. Soon, no doubt, the sales information will be a chip embedded in a handshake. Meanwhile, we engage in 'networking clusters' and 'speed dating' and breakout sessions, not to mention colloquia on diverse, often arcane, themes.

Yet we must ask: has the arts market outlived its usefulness? Have new digital platforms made touring partly redundant? Is the rapid, borderless exchange of artists and their practice, and the worldwide experience of co-productions, residencies and other collaboration, making the idea of moving whole shows around unnecessary? Isn't the world simply saturated with contemporary dance, physical theatre and new music?

Everywhere, these markets are searching for means to adapt to external change as well as to find new ways to be distinctive. APAM is seeking to reinvent itself from an intensive, biennial, four-day conference to an elongated 'process' with intrusions into a range of pre-existing events around the country. So, the urge for renewal is in the air. But change to what? Where might it end? And, as lawyers used to enquire, *cui bono*?

Because there are external factors which impact on such events. The evolution of communication technologies and social media, environmental issues and global financial crises are among them. They can be challenges and opportunities. In addition, the way the performing arts do business—and where—is changing. Traditional markets may no longer have the capacity to deliver as in the past. New markets may offer—or seem to offer—new prospects. A basket of strategies, including the vital component of personal relations, on-ground knowledge and on-site representation will have to be part of the mix, whatever new models emerge.

This paper questions some of the assumptions underlying the notion of a 'market'; the role that government agencies have played in advocating, enabling and even owning such events; and seeks to evaluate some of their pros, cons and notable shortcomings. Yet, there are also other pathways which artists have pursued, including those being trialled in Australia and elsewhere which we need to note.

1. What are performing arts markets? What do they do and why do we need them?

The bottom line of performing arts markets is touring. It can be dressed up in many ways, but if artists and companies did not feel compelled to move their product around the country or the world, there would be no need for them. Equally, if all nations stayed at home and played to their own backyard there would be no world trade. We would inhabit a kind of Trumpian subsistence economy in which each parish did its own thing and exchanged only insults with its neighbours.

Central to my topic is the idea of cultural contact. When people meet in market they exchange not just goods and services but the customs and beliefs that shaped them. Friendships are forged. These processes are largely invisible until some extraordinary fusion results. As the great, and today rather neglected, historical geographer Oskar Spate remarked: 'there are no bills of lading for ideas.'[4]

It also comes down to motivation. Almost no-one makes money by overseas touring. Break-even is the best we can hope for and that is usually achieved by some form of subsidy. Nonetheless, being able to demonstrate earned income from abroad can be psychologically significant and important as an argument to funding agencies.

However, money is not the only aim. Extending the life of a work in ways which cannot be sustained in a small domestic market has both artistic and organisational benefits. Putting work in front of a culturally or socially different audience and seeking their response is also vital for many artists. One can also never entirely discount sheer vanity. Who doesn't want to say they had a standing ovation in New York? So the measurements may be varied and complex.

To market to market

Notwithstanding these endowments, the performing arts market has struck root in only certain parts of the world. Conceived in North America, the idea spread with success to Australia and Asia and less so to Latin America. It has functioned sporadically in Africa and gained minor traction in Europe though there have been some variants there on the theme.

At its rawest end, there is APAP. Begun in the US in the 1950s with just 29 college presenters participating, it grew to today's behemoth of 1600 active members in every art form across the country and around the world. Its annual jamboree is held in New York's City each January. This is the version that most represents the arts supermarket that is so distasteful to many. Yet it succeeds and business is done. At its gentler end, there are those smaller or medium scale activities such as Australia's APAM, Japan's Performing Arts Meeting (TPAM)[5] and Canada's CINARS which exhibit many of the same features and opportunities. There, in all probability, less hard business has been conducted but more genuine connection made. In those three instances, set in smaller trading environments, markets strive to overcome 'disadvantages' of location and distance by offering an intensive periodic array of local wares.

It is possible, however, that the model only truly works where the marketplace is huge, the product extensive, the intermediaries—such as agents and presenters—highly organised and pervasive and where all that is accompanied by advanced negotiating skill and experience. As well, in order to have an effective trade fair one must have buyers *and* sellers. It is arguable that in APAM, while there have been a number of buyers, there has never really been selling. The work has been displayed but not sold. There can also be something rather artificial about the international buyers, often lured by subsidised travel, accommodation and free registration (and perhaps the chance of a side trip to the Great Barrier Reef). One sometimes asks how genuinely engaged they have been. While there has been a hard core of regulars, over 50 per cent come once and never return. Distance, timing and cost obviously play a part, but equally the invitees have not always been wisely chosen.

Another question remains: everywhere, festivals and other presenting organisations are increasingly commissioning and co-producing internationally. The Director of the Sydney Festival, Wesley Enoch, claimed at its 2019 launch that his event was now the largest event commissioning body in Australia with 46 active commissions at this time.[6] How do developments like that relate to the maintenance of a physical market? It is instructive that none of the North American events is called a 'market'. CINARS is a 'Conference for the Theatre Arts', TPAM and PAMS are 'meetings'. APAP is usually just called 'Arts Presenters', WAA in the US West is an 'Alliance', PAE on America's Eastern seaboard is an 'Exchange,' and so on. Even APAM is now presenting itself as a 'meeting'. The final report on APAM's Brisbane cycle noted the goal of 'shifting the focus of the market from being transactional in nature to one that is embedded in notions of conversation, collaboration, exchange, and networking.'[7]

Nevertheless, most observers today would acknowledge that these events have a networking and relationship-building purpose alongside their buying and selling role. While there is concern with the narrowness of what 'market' might mean, many feel that it has been useful to add new dimensions to the program in order to facilitate what might be called 'curated conversations'. Such developments aim to meet the need for more emphasis on international collaborations and forging creative partnerships than the previous open-ended, freewheeling encounters could provide.

However, there is also concern at the diminution of the essential trading element. It is expensive to participate, so the pressure is on to make it attendance-productive. To this uncertainty has been added a kind of *faux* conference framework at which the common aims and issues of the performing arts sector could be discussed. Since, until recently, APAM was the only gathering that brought the Australian performing arts together every two years, that social aspect had grown in visibility. The new APAM format is likely to diminish that, and the more dynamic Performing Arts Connections' (PAC)[8] annual conference may in part replace it. All of these have emerged on the reasonable premise that everyone in the sector has something to share, be it product or experience, information or ideas. So it may be that once more barter has become as important as trade.

At the same time, we are far from alone in worrying about how to stand out in the crowd. Competition comes not only from other producers but also from other markets and mechanisms, notably in our own Asia-Pacific region. Most of the organisations that manage these events have contemplated a rethink of the template that ranges from the cosmetic to the radical. Abandoning many of the conventional aspects of a trade fair, they've opted for limited showcasing and big conversational formats, intensive encounters, laboratories, and highly curated packages of experience. Time will tell where these will go.

2. Common characteristics

Arts markets form part of what Frank Moorhouse neatly called *Conference-ville* in his book of that name[9]—a place where otherwise-rational people behave in unnatural ways so as to endorse a collective belief in group conformity, solidarity. Recently, this writer attended the Performing Arts Network New Zealand (PANNZ) in Auckland, Aotearoa's annual bunfight on the international arts market circuit.[10] On day one, delegates were shepherded by garishly dressed actors through the rear access of the Town Hall into an auditorium, which, by the way, had perfectly serviceable front doors. We were then directed onto the stage where a selection of hats and garb lay about rather in the manner of the 'dress-up' box of unlamented Yuletide charades. We were invited to festoon ourselves for a series of group photos.

The purpose was never explained. Everyone participated, no doubt for fear of offending some antique Kiwi ritual whose significance is lost in the Long White Cloud. It is not the worst thing that has happened to me at an arts market. (That would be the time at APAP when a woman from a children's choir in a more than ordinarily reductive mid-Western state sought to sequester me in her lair to sell her little treasures.)

I mention such matters only to stress that these are

curious assemblies, albeit well-intended. They exhibit something of the church fête: full of fierce bonhomie, backslapping, manufactured enthusiasm and invasion of personal space. (A distinguished Canadian presenter attending APAM recounts once being pursued into the ladies' lavatory at the Adelaide Festival Centre by an overzealous Australian producer determined to make a sale.) Also, anyone who has been to these congregations comes away severely hugged out.

I referenced 'fête' above and it was not entirely throwaway. For at arts markets there are usually stalls, rather like those which once proffered toffee apples and hoopla for parish causes and can still be found at trade fairs promoting travel destinations or farm machinery. All such arts markets have what is often called the contact/exhibition room. There one is confronted by serried ranks of booths whose denizens (and I have been one) lie in wait to trap the passer-by with information, sweetened by chocolates, mints, badges and even, on one occasion in Montreal, a fairy floss machine. All this is to secure five minutes' chat about their dance company, string quartet, circus act or burlesque show. Australian colleagues and I once did a roaring trade there with mass-produced clip-on koalas. Strange how potent cheap ideas can be, as Noel Coward almost said. These stalls are sibylline caves of prophesy and persuasion, so beware. The magic lamp of a USB is pressed into our palm, business cards and promises of future contact exchanged and the buyer, bewared, moves on. This is not to say there is no deeper engagement.

Many sit to watch a video on a discreetly positioned laptop; or view a show-reel on a TV monitor. Genuine interest may well result. The booths are also sites for appointments with those who truly wish to trade and there is skill involved in securing the deal under these conditions. But in the end success is achieved mostly after long-standing connection between artist manager/producer and presenter. Rarely is it spur-of-the-moment. A presenter (and I have been one) is fresh meat on the hoof in these places. The more aggressive the market, the more endangered the target.

Above all there are the showcases, long or short, to which the myriads tear from room to room or from site to site on foot, in buses or in the Northern winter climes skidding through ice and snow in a Montreal November blizzard, a chilly Manhattan January or contrariwise through a desiccating Adelaide at 40°C in February. They hope to catch 6 x 15 minutes of bleeding chunks of contemporary dance or physical theatre. More happily, they may see one whole evening performance of something rich and rare in a Fringe venue under a staircase or in a room with the allure of a toilet block.

To be sure, it is not all just about making a sale. Many register for these markets to catch up; to see what's what; who's who; and what the trends may be across the industry. That is the valuable, perhaps invaluable, part of the experience and one which we in Australia may soon be in danger of casting away through heightened sectional interests and whose loss, under the new APAM regime, we may come to regret. It is also about a sense of belonging to something bigger than our small, if essential, export opportunity or just filling a gap in next year's program.

It was not long ago that we travelled to these markets laden down with cartons of CDs, printed flyers, VHS tapes and much else. Today, it is all about the website and the smart phone. Soon, no doubt, we will offer cheap spectacles with built-in VR. But pressing the flesh remains central to the act. However, the lack of impedimenta today has gradually meant more time for other things. Talkfest has proliferated at the arts market on matters ranging from the speculative to the practical, from community engagement in remote and regional venues; to work visas in the US and the functioning of the Schengen Treaty Zone. And I have rarely been to a market at which talk about new ticketing software is not a feature.

We hope that delegates go away improved or informed or with joy in their hearts from experiences such as these. Sometimes I have wondered if it might not be more productive were greater time in the schedule allowed for sitting and dreaming. Nevertheless, one can still find oneself wandering in circles looking for an appointment with someone known only from a postage stamp-sized photo in the guide book or, increasingly, on an app.

Unsurprisingly , the motivation for being there and crowding the day varies hugely from country to country, culture to culture. North Americans are better organised and often hunt in packs. In the Asia/Pacific we are more lone wolves. Latin Americans are, counter-intuitively perhaps, reserved and courteous. But everywhere there is an undercurrent of desperation, often leading to disappointment. It's like the dismay at not catching a fish the first time, before realising that it takes a while to get the knack.

Then, as with any conference anywhere, there are the so-called plenary sessions in a big hall where some expert from across the water is hired to give the word on a burning topic. I have rarely found these alluring in advance or satisfying in retrospect; but it is possible that I am one of those who might have slept through the Sermon on the Mount. And on the matter of feeding the multitude, about the best idea of any of these markets was the practice which the Quebec conference CINARS enjoyed for many years of holding a differently themed breakfast each morning. These were often focussed on a country or region with a representative talking, at not too great length, about what we might see in their showcases or the art forms they represented. It was at a time of day when most felt alert and the talks helped inform what was to follow. CINARS was often the source of the best conference ideas and to my mind had long been the outstanding performing arts market, as well as the model for many others worldwide in terms of scale, civility and quality of offerings.

Inevitably, quality is the key factor and again over the decades CINARS has been far and away best practice in 'curating', to use the *mot du jour*. While like all markets, it is primarily a platform for its home-grown product, CINARS it has been broadly international in its invitation to artists from other lands to showcase. Thereby, it found a balance, between the local and the imported, and in that way enriched its attendance by presenters, who were equally diverse. Apart from a loose partnership with New Zealand and a very occasional gesture to Singapore, Australia has never been as open or generous. As a result, it has never built a loyal following or as engaged an attendance. I hope that whatever succeeds the seemingly now defunct former APAM model will be more inviting.

Making the match

Renting a booth is, by contrast, open to anyone in either system but the dominating presence of state and federal agencies in the contact room effectively stifled that mechanism in Australia; and with it also the visibility of independent arts managers and small-scale producers here, which for a short time in the 1990s looked promising. APAM had also been rather too obsessed with distributing its showcasing favours evenly across our various jurisdictions without equivalent attention to quality. The end result has been a failure to pick export 'winners' or match them with presenter demand. This has resulted in an often low level of showcases and that in turn has eroded delegate loyalty.

None of these aspects is new or unusual. All are features of industrial or academic gatherings everywhere and for whatever purpose. What makes it curious in this context is that the arts, which pride themselves on being innovative and cutting edge, have so slavishly followed such antiquated formats.

There is, however, one slightly original element of the performing arts market, largely confined to the US and which more than anything emphasises how these events serve to commodify those arts. That is the group booking phenomenon or booking consortia. On the face of it, they take a rational approach to making the touring of work of interest to more than one presenter, and more efficient in time and resources. If six arts centres in neighbouring locations can book a show within a given period and create economies of scale in terms of travel, freight, remount costs, bump-in days' insurances and the like, of course it makes sense to collaborate. Maybe a group discount can be negotiated. The Centres get a show at a lower price. The artists get repeat business and maybe less on-road wear and tear. What, as they say, is not to like?

In the US these consortia, often based in a state or in a group of contiguous states, book like this consistently. The Australian market lacks that precise method, though the now defunct Long Paddock/Blue Heelers scheme operated on similar principles and with similar results. The outcome is not the choice of good art but of convenient art. It is, or was, a numbers game. The result has too often been a dumbing down in the selection of work so that the most popular (or should one say populist?) product prevailed; and thereby excluded more interesting work that could not command the number of presenter bids to make the tour cost-efficient. It led instead to a progressive narrowing of the range of artists presented, especially in regional centres, and thereby reduced access to the very touring mechanisms that would benefit the small-to-medium sector. Since in Australia the pot of gold at the end of the Long Paddock was access to the Federal Government's Playing Australia fund, this was lock-out, twice over.

But wait, there's more: the closing dinner and the Awards ceremony! Again, this began with our American cousins giving out prizes for being the best in arts management: sponsorship, leadership or sheer longevity. A bit of fun, a few speeches between the main course and the dessert. Australia has put its own spin on them. To pursue for a moment the bush analogy, PAC has the Drover Awards and the Touring Legend as well as Best Arts Centre and so forth. You have to be there to appreciate the full thrill.

Too much government?

Speaking of thrills, we come now to politicians and their role. By that I don't mean ministers, MPs or mayors who occasionally turn up at arts markets, and proffer welcoming remarks in the conference program. I refer to the manner in which, in this country, government arts agencies have maintained a stranglehold on the market mode in ways that have been utterly unhelpful. APAM is again the prime example. For many years it was titled 'the Australia Council's Arts Market' and it took quite some effort to prise their fingers off the brand. Below the line, they are still there.

Until its last real outing in Brisbane, those who entered the ever-diminishing exhibition room were greeted by stand after stand of State arts agencies nesting the chicks of their local companies. By 2010 in Adelaide eleven stands were occupied by local or overseas government agencies and only nine by independent producers.[11] It was a bad and misleading look and did nothing to help promote the individual qualities of the companies so lodged in their respective government bosoms. Regrettably, we now see that same phenomenon in other markets, including CINARS. Sad, as Donald Trump would tweet. While the dead hand of government intervention is rarely far from the arts in the Anglosphere, other than in the US, it is depressing to see the Scandinavian and Benelux countries getting in on this same act to a similar dismal end.

Today, although little new or different in market land, there is much that is familiar from other such events across the trading world. It may be that buying and selling have always defaulted to the same patterns since craftspeople first set out to sell their pots in Nineveh. Pehaps, like Mortein, we should stick to a good thing when we're on it, but question whether it is the only possible good thing. It couldn't go astray, could it?

3. Where did they come from? North America and Australasia

As with many innovations in showbiz, the arts market began in the United States with APAP. From there it spread north, where Canada, being Canada, evolved two events: a Francophone version, CINARS and an essentially Anglophone version, the Canadian Arts Presenting Association (CAPACOA)[12]. Across North America regional copies proliferated. Gradually, the idea was picked up around the world, eventually working its way into the Asia-Pacific, Africa and even to Europe.

APAP (USA)

However, the 800-pound gorilla was always APAP, the American national service, advocacy and membership organisation for presenters of the performing arts. It hosts the annual APAP|NYC conference—the world's most brutal convening for the arts industry, which began in the 1950s when college and university concert managers focused on the needs of professional performing arts on campuses. It started at the Wisconsin Union Theater and during the 1960s and 70s expanded to cover a variety of organisations, prompting the body to change its name in 1973 to the Association of College, University and Community Arts Administrators (ACUCAA). By the mid-1980s, colleges and universities no longer dominated, but the organisation's reach continued to grow. It became the Association of Performing Arts Presenters in 1988.

Today, APAP represents the non-profit and for-profit sectors of the presenting and touring industry in the US and internationally, with member organisations from all fifty states and at least fifty countries. It has no fear of combining the subsidised and commercial. They include large performing arts centres in major cities, outdoor festivals, rural community-focused organisations, academic institutions, individual artists, and artist managers and booking agents. It is from this extraordinary and daunting enterprise that the performing arts market worldwide takes its form and to some degree its nature.

Of course, APAP is not the only international body based in the United States that exhibits some form of market. The decades-old International Society for the Performing Arts (ISPA)[13] which is basically an association of arts managers, has long included in its bi-annual conferences a modest market activity. It is mentioned here because its mid-year conference moves from country to country and through that the contamination spreads.

CINARS (Canada)

In Australian arts consciousness, the next such event and, in terms of scale a more tractable version, was supplied by Montreal's CINARS. Since 1984, it has presented one of the most important international performing arts gatherings anywhere, with around 1900 delegates hailing from 54 countries including over four hundred show presenters. Over a week, more than 170 shows from Quebec, Canada and elsewhere occupy the city's numerous stages, while an exhibition hall with workshops and networking events teems with participants.

After 18 editions, the CINARS Biennale is today the most globally minded of all the arts markets. Uniquely situated in a bilingual environment, it has that great advantage over its United States peers in forming a natural bridge between Europe and North America; and increasingly has looked in the other direction, to the Asia-Pacific region. No US market has ever achieved that. And though it did not start out that way, CINARS maintains a year-long presence abroad through Quebec On Stage, by which every year it arranges, along with Quebec arts companies and agents, joint attendance in other international markets. APAP, by contrast, is almost suffocatingly parochial.

CAPACOA

By no means in the same league as CINARS, CAPACOA, founded in 1985, serves a similar purpose in AngloCanada though at a more domestic level. It began in 1988 by hosting an annual itinerant conference for the sector, which brought together cultural entrepreneurs and key industry stakeholders across national and international performing arts sectors. In 2016, CAPACOA reshaped its model by holding its event in conjunction with the CINARS Biennale with which it is strategically coming together.

Regional USA

Given the scale of the North American market as well is its land mass, it is no surprise that regional clones of APAP should arise. In terms of format and activity there is little to choose among them. Some are more effective than others, but all fulfil essentially the same trade-oriented function. For instance, for over 35 years Arts Northwest[14] has been serving Oregon, Washington State and Idaho; and in 1991 started rotating between the three states to a variety of cities. Western Arts Alliance (WAA)[15] is by an order of magnitude the most adventurous and energetic of the regionals covering, as its name suggests, most of the West Coast. Begun in 1967 for presenters located largely in California, the Alliance of Western Colleges for Cultural Presentations today has over four hundred members, and around a thousand participants at its annual conference, with two hundred artists, managers and agents exhibiting. By contrast The Performing Arts Exchange (PAE)[16] managed by South Arts, hosted in an eastern city each year and now over forty years old, may well be the most supine. It is the primary marketplace and forum for performing arts' presenting and touring in the south-eastern states. Likewise, Arts Midwest[17] covers a nine-state service region, which includes Illinois, Indiana, Iowa, Michigan, Minnesota, North Dakota, Ohio, South Dakota and Wisconsin. Through strategic alliances, its key programs also reach into Arkansas, Kansas, Missouri, Nebraska, Oklahoma, Pennsylvania, Texas, and beyond.

While most of these smaller conferences serve geographic areas, some have a more thematic approach. Prime among these is International Performing Arts for Youth (IPAY)[18] held each January in Philadelphia. It is the premier event in North America dedicated to 'promoting international performing arts for young audiences' and is highly regarded by youth theatre companies in Australia who over recent years have done extremely well from showcasing there.

Australasia

Curiously, the Asia-Pacific region was the next to be bitten by the market bug. In fact, APAM was first cab off the rank in this part of the world and aimed to 'increase international and national touring opportunities for Australian contemporary performing arts groups and artists'. That largely stands today.[19] Note two things about this goal: first is the inclusion of the word 'national' although APAM has almost exclusively focused its guns on international; and second that there is no reference to the scale of work to be promoted i.e. nothing about the small-to-medium sector. Like many other mechanisms seeking to promote and sell Australian product abroad, APAM was largely about the Australian Government intervening in what might otherwise have been a free-for-all. Somewhere along the line it also became, inevitably, about government setting the market agenda: who's in; who's out; what are the market conditions and what are the mechanisms to influence that? No chance of arm's-length there.

Thirteen APAM editions have been held to date in Canberra (2), Adelaide (8) and most recently Brisbane (3). The site and its management have been conventionally allocated through a Request for Tender from the Australia Council. The result has been a partnership between the Council and whichever State agency was selected. The actual operations are delegated by contract to a third party. (Most recently the state body is Creative Victoria.) But now we are promised a whole new paradigm for APAM's operations.

Whatever one thinks of this market mechanism and/ or its strengths and weaknesses, APAM has achieved a lot since its inception and has continued, until recently, to maintain a strong international reputation. Numerous tours have been booked and a number of Australian artists have secured international representation through the market.[20] Above all, APAM has been a major networking opportunity and, as with all such gatherings, it is likely that much of the 'business' is serendipitous or at least below the radar of the official program. Beyond anecdote, however, that aspect is harder to gauge. Even with feedback from participants and scrutiny of tour grants as analysed over the years in formal reports, accurate tracking of the outcomes has been subjective and elusive.

What's more, international attendance has varied. There was a steady rise over the early life of the Market, with a particularly large increase in 2002 from under 30 in 1994 to a spike of just under 150 in 2002. There was then something of a plateau up to the last Adelaide edition.[21]

The picture thereafter is harder to read. For instance it is noteworthy that while international delegates rose from 186 in 2014 to 196 in 2016 and then to 273 in 2018, Australian delegates declined from 441 to 407 in the same period. Even after deducting the NZ contingent of usually between 30 and 40 delegates, it is startling to see how large a proportion of internationals were in some degree 'supported' by APAM to attend. That rose from 88 in 2016 to 102 in 2018 (plus contributions in Asia by DFAT and various of the bilateral bodies such as the Australia Korea Foundation). The picture is further blurred when reports reveal that in 2018 of the total 680 attendance there were 218 complimentary registrations. Now there can be excellent reasons for all of those actions individually, but taken together they do suggest an artificiality in the market which at the very least must call into question how genuine a trading post it is.[22]

Conferencing

Yet around the original export proposition for APAM has grown an *omnium gatherum* of the performing arts in Australasia. In 2018 there were 680 delegates of whom 407 were from Australia.[23] That is a remarkable record and greatly exceeds those who appear to be formally engaged in the buying and selling.

Part of this informal activity clusters around what the event means for the *national* touring scene in Australia. Certainly, in quality and range of work on offer, APAM fulfilled a need not met by the now discontinued domestic showcases of Long/Cyber Paddock and the like. Case studies in the in 2014–2018 Brisbane APAM report suggest that some domestic touring has been engendered through it, though the picture is too indistinct to allow a reliable assessment.[24] Since in any market, buyers, including international buyers, are often to some degree sellers, there has always been a case for formalising this previously unacknowledged dimension of APAM and providing properly for it, as was recommended in an earlier report.[25]

APAM has now been relocated to Melbourne, working nationally and for the first time with a year-round staffed base. The new proactive operating model has an expanded function. It recognises that

> *Australian artists and arts organisations are well-connected, savvy and resilient market-leaders working across a spectrum of international engagement strategies: touring, co-commissioning, collaboration and residencies.*[26]

In the past, it was all about touring. Now the role of APAM is seen to be more about deepening relationships and fostering opportunities for exchange, reciprocal connections, and hospitality. Of course, it has always attempted some of that. The question now is whether the shiny new model will succeed any better than the old.

APAM now sees itself as having three functions: the year-round presence to facilitate visitors to Australia; hosting one or two annual gatherings at established festivals around Australia to replace the previous biennial market; and providing market intelligence for and about contemporary Australian performance. At the time of writing, two of these new events have been announced for 2020: AsiaTopa: Melbourne in February and at the Darwin Festival in August. Rumour has it that the Perth Festival 2021 will be next. The organisers believe that increasing the number of APAM events in a diversity of contexts will encourage overseas delegates to visit performing arts communities around the country.

That remains to be demonstrated. It is also not clear why an arts intelligence service should work any better today than it did for recent predecessors, or what lessons were learned from their failures. Perhaps the only thing that is really apparent in the new order is increased emphasis on Indigenous performing arts. But whether that welcome initiative will in itself be sufficient to attract international delegates also remains to be seen.

As well, all of the mainland states conduct for domestic purposes their own mini arts markets. These focus on regional touring and bringing together performing arts centres and producers, both for-profit and not-for-profit, for whom they represent vital touring circuits. They include WA Showcase organised by CircuitWest[27], Showcase SA, organised by the SA Presenters Association[28] and a very low key event called simply Salon, managed by NSW's Arts on Tour.[29] Queensland Touring Showcase is organised by arTour[30] and Showcase Victoria by the Victorian Association of Performing Arts Centres (VAPAC).[31] Their history has been uneven and each has tended to operate on a different basis reflecting the circumstances of their environments.[32]

In some ways in response to what had become a plethora of domestic touring networks and managements, in 2015 PAC created Performing Arts Exchange (PAX). It is a national two-day event which in 2019 attracted 292 delegates, a record thus far. The quality of its showcases and pitch sessions is generally high and there would seem to be agreement that this event, held with the PAC annual conference in a different town or city each year, is finding favour with its far-flung constituency. Business is done between producers and presenters although such is the imbalance of the Australian scene there are never enough of the latter to satisfy the former. Depending on the outcome of the new look APAM, it is interesting to see that this alternative has emerged and could with effective leadership take on a greater role in bringing the Australian industry regularly together for its periodic powwow.

PANNZ New Zealand

Across the pond for the last ten years we have had APAM's younger and smaller sister PANNZ, which supports the New Zealand professional performing arts sector and aims to encourage a sustainable performing arts touring network there. Its activity includes running the annual PANNZ Arts Market and Tour-Makers' National Touring Agency. It does not have a big international dimension though it is often aligned with Creative New Zealand's *Te manu ka tau*[33] which invites international delegates who often travel on from one of the Australian events and, as its name suggests, involves an all- too-brief immersion in Maori or Pacific Island culture.

The PANNZ Arts Market was launched in 1999, in partnership with Entertainment Venues Association of New Zealand (EVANZ). The Arts Market is the sole marketplace for performing arts in New Zealand and has grown from a one-day market featuring eleven works to a three-day event featuring more than fifty works. It is now one of the most important industry events on the New Zealand calendar and alternates between Auckland and Wellington at the time of their respective International Arts Festivals.

4. Further afield

Somewhat later than in Australia, the arts market phenomenon spread to Asia, notably East and South-east Asia. The variety is too great to detail all, so highlights must suffice to give a sense of what has happened, and offer some background to the range of competition that Australia faces in this regard.

TPAM is the oldest performing arts platform in Asia, celebrating 24 years in 2019. Launched in Tokyo as Tokyo Performing Arts Market, it moved to Yokohama in 2011 and at that time reduced its name to the acronym only. About four hundred international professionals from 41 countries/regions and 480 from across Japan took part in the 2019 edition. Following an international trend, most of the programs were opened to the 27,000-strong public audience. Today the event incorporates 'TPAM Direction,' a performance program that reflects the currents of contemporary performing arts in Asia and the world; 'TPAM Exchange,' a meeting program where festivals, venues and arts organisations across the world get together; and 'TPAM Fringe,' an open-call program for emerging, and experienced, artists.

CIPAE, formerly known as CIPAC or CIPAF, is also an annual event held in Beijing by the China Association of Performing Arts (CAPA).[34] Since its first edition in 2001, CIPAE has attracted over 1,500 participants a year for four days to showcases, pitches, forums, and the inevitable exhibition room. CIPAE has become the most important performing arts market in China, though, given the somewhat restricted nature of the market concept in the People's Republic, it is not always clear what that means.

With support from the Ministry of Culture, Sports and Tourism, Korea Arts Management Service has been hosting the Performing Arts Market in Seoul (PAMS)[35] each October since 2005 to coincide with the Seoul International Arts Festival. It exhibits the familiar range of showcases of selected Korean performing arts, booths, forums and networking programs. In 2019 PAMS comprehensively curated its networking (some would say over-curated) so that participants could enjoy more opportunity for exchange. Again with the aim of providing a freer meeting environment, the dreaded contact room replaced the sheltered booths with an open space with tables. The new-look PAMS also selected fewer items for PAMS 'Choice'—its showcase program—where for the first time some works were presented full-length. PAMS has also diversified its pitching program.

In Singapore the original arts market was convened by the Esplanade Arts Centre from 2003, ran a few editions and was then converted into an artist platform, ConversAsians, which in turn expired some years later. In 2010 and 2011 there was another event called Live!, arranged by Koelnmesse. It was planned to run with the support of the Singapore Tourism Board but was terminated due to a bleak economic outlook. Why was it that, in this most mercantile of cities, the market model that had flourished in other, seemingly less fertile, ground, could not long be sustained?

Then there is the relatively new Taiwanese networking platform known simply as ADAM,[36] co-organised by the Taipei Performing Arts Centre (TPAC) and Taipei Culture Foundation. It focuses on partnership and for that reason stands out a little from the crowd. Interestingly, it is also open to connections with other arts networks and organisations including those outside the region. Somewhat surprisingly the acronym actually stands, not inappropriately, for 'Asia Discovers Asia Meeting (for Contemporary Performance)'. Also, the prime components of ADAM are a three-week multi-art-form exchange lab led by four curators from different countries and built around a theme: The Kitchen—a series of works-in-progress for presenters of projects seeded at the preceding ADAM—and Assembly, the four-day meeting of presenters/producers.

Bangkok's BIPAM[37] where again the AM also stands for Arts Meeting, aims to make the Thai capital a platform for regional and international exchange. In a way it is more conference than overtly a market. It hopes to become South-east Asia's performing arts launch pad. With each edition the organisers commit to exhibiting a more comprehensive view of the ASEAN patch. In 2013 Indonesia made a short-lived attempt with a market called IPAM to achieve this goal but without success.

Africa has made a less obvious response to the trading concept than other continents. It is potentially an enormous market, though compared with other parts of the world its professional performing arts networking remains underdeveloped and its infrastructure is unevenly spread. The first overt market event the Abidjan Market for Performing Arts (MASA)[38] emerged, not entirely surprisingly, in a former French colony, the Côte d'Ivoire. The concept was developed in 1990 at a conference of the Ministers of Culture and Francophonie, but the event itself was not formally realised until 1993. In 1998, the MASA was declared 'an international organization for the promotion of African performing arts' and in 1999 an agreement was signed between the Côte d'Ivoire Government and the MASA, that established its headquarters in Abidjan. Over the last twenty years, the MASA has become an important showcase for African contemporary creation both about the region and across the nations of the region; and it has added significant commercial value to artistic groups and their production.

At the same time the East African Performing Arts Market (DOADOA),[39] which presented its eighth edition in 2019, acts as a platform for professional African networking and joint learning; and its territory is much further south in the continent than the MASA. DOADOA brings together stakeholders and links people, organisations, businesses, knowledge and technology—essentially of the East African creative sector. Like the MASA, DOADOA is also a joint initiative of leading creative entrepreneurs, who had joined forces to develop the market for performing arts in East Africa and to provide an annual platform to bring together various stakeholders across the industry and forge links. Bayimba Cultural Foundation is one of the initiators and works closely with Sarakasi Trust (Kenya), Phat! Entertainment (Kenya), Ketebul Music (Kenya), Busara Promotions (Tanzania), Caravan Records (Tanzania), KigaliUp (Rwanda) and Selam Music (Ethiopia).

Europe

Europe is the most dense and layered market for the live performing arts in the world. Its scale offers many and varied pathways to the sale, exchange and movement of performing arts activity. Its relative proximity to the Middle East and North Africa, and the residual ties of former colonial powers in those regions, also ensures that European interests are spread not only over their own continent but also linked to their neighbourhood.

All of that adds to its complexity and the enormous range of initiatives which at any one time are operating in those markets. For those reasons among others, Europe has found itself much less reliant on the annual or biennial market mechanism, although these undoubtedly exist in such as WOMEX in World Music, the Venice Biennale in the visual arts, the Cannes Film Festival, and Tarrega in street theatre. Europe also tends to operate through less structured means at almost below the radar, through congregations such as the Informal European Theatre Managers (IETM) to give it its now-almost-redundant name, or the biennial Ice Hot in the contemporary dance world.

Nevertheless, there are a few standard market events which would be recognisable to the aficionados of APAP, APAM or TPAM in their respective territories. Perhaps most notable, given its location, is Rumania's Sibiu Performing Arts Market.[40] Since its first edition in 1997 this event—unique in Central and South-east Europe—has been associated with the Sibiu International Theatre Festival (FITS) and is the product of the Festival's aim to provide opportunities to all artists, cultural operators, performing arts institutions and cultural networks in the region; and to make contact with significant producers from around the world.

On the other side of the continent—and in its own way outside the European heartland—is Ireland's International Theatre eXchange (ITX), established in 1994.[41] ITX is presented by the Irish Theatre Institute primarily as an opportunity for Irish theatre artists and companies, programmed during the Dublin International Theatre Festival, to develop their networks and explore collaborations with programmers interested in presenting Irish work to their audiences. Compared with many such events ITX is intimate. A small number of specially invited international presenters and producers experience a weekend program of showcasing and networking. These guests experience a diverse range of Irish performance, including a curated pitching Session, a series of rehearsed works 'in development' and a program of Irish Festival productions.

Meanwhile from the Iberian Peninsula (though not actually located on it) is Spain/Portugal's MAPAS Mercado Cultural.[42] This is very new. Its third edition took place in Santa Cruz de Tenerife (Canary Islands), in July 2019. MAPAS is the first professional performing arts market in the region and acts as a meeting place for music, theatre, dance, circus and street artists from South Europe, Latin America and Africa; and those in charge of programming, cultural spaces, festivals and other events worldwide.

Latin America

Perhaps because it's closest to the US, Mexico was the first country in this region to host a performing arts market and inevitably drew on the models created further north. Strictly speaking, it has had three such events in succession, all of which have been, thus far at least, relatively short lived. The first occurred in Mexico City in 1993 and was called MERCARTES. It was a huge occasion with a myriad of full-length live performances by some of the country's most important performing arts companies. It featured discussion, a very large exhibition hall and significant international participation. Regrettably, it enjoyed just one outing.

In 2004 a second attempt was made, this time under the auspices of FONCA, an agency of the Federal Ministry of Culture. Again, the market, called appropriately *Puerta de las Américas* or Gateway to the Americas, manifested all of the standard features of such events. It survived for some years on an annual basis until succeeded by yet another version called ENARTES.[43] This one ran until 2018 when, as a consequence of a change in government policy, its last outing took place. The event's aim is/was to promote Mexican performances on a national and international platform in addition to showcasing cultural and professional enterprises, inspiring participant creativity and encouraging innovation in performance.

By contrast was the success of Ventana Internacional de las Artes or International Window on the Arts (VIA)[44] held in association with the biennial Ibero-American Theatre Festival in Bogotá, Colombia. Though much smaller and more focused than the Mexican or other comparable, periodic events scattered around the continent, VIA has been more consistent and persistent. Launched in 2004, and celebrating its ninth edition in 2018, it was designed as a business centre for the exchange of predominantly Colombian work, and has attracted programmers from around the world. The results suggest that it has been successful in promoting export to other countries not only in Latin America but in Europe, Australasia and Asia. Given the scale of the accompanying festival with its large component of local and other Latin American productions, there has been little need to develop a special showcase program for VIA, though approximately fifty theatre companies actively participate in the relentless speed-dating round-tables and other opportunities for interchange.

Coda

It is characteristic of a continent which has traditionally been the net importer of structured arts activity, that organisers of many of these events in Latin America tend to see such markets as an opportunity to redress the balance, to level the playing field, so to speak. A platform is provided which enables local artists to compete with overseas artists and companies, who are often seen as having a significant advantage in their own market and in the world. That is emblematic of many markets distant from the North American and European cultural hegemony. In that context, networking is critical. But in Latin America producers tend not to view it simply as a matter of 'closing the deal' but of getting close enough to international promoters to make a deal possible.

One Mexican authority observed:

> *You can only love something if you see it. Digital reproduction is fine, but personal encounter is more powerful and that's particularly true in the Latin*

American ambience. But the other really significant element is the way in which it builds confidence, in the artist and in the producer. To be able to go to a programmer and feel that you are communicating with them on equal terms.[45]

These are observations that could be made in any part of the world about performing arts markets. We have heard them many times in Australia. However, it was particularly instructive to hear them articulated in such a contrasting cultural and economic environment. It was at once a measure of how globalised all these issues have become and at the same time offered a potent example of the risks of commodification in them.

5. What is the scene today?

The Showcase

Despite the formulaic conference-like nature of much of the arts trading phenomenon, many events have also moved into other formats and/or acquired other characteristics. For instance, within the 'talkfest' domain, the panel is ubiquitous as are the pseudo-relaxed armchair chats—the interview you have when you aren't having an interview. Then there is the graphic facilitation where artisans illustrate, with numbers, swirls and geometric forms on white boards, what is being said in a session. What happens to these after the delegates have gone for lunch is a mystery. Perhaps somewhere there is a repository reserved for later ages to archaeologically retrieve our thoughts like the frozen head of Albert Finney in *Cold Lazarus?*[46] Or are they merely discarded as the detritus of another conversational gimmick?

At the same time, many of the organisations that run these usually annual, sometimes biennial, gatherings have themselves broadened into other fields. Whereas they started as meetings of minds and trading posts, today many invest in other activity. APAP, for instance, offers several grant programs for its members to recognise outstanding and innovative practice. Others have scholarships and internships for emerging managers and producers, usually recent graduates from the proliferating arts management courses. These provide experience, often in another country, giving insights into the path ahead to those who might in time find themselves on one or other side of the trade fair fence, selling or buying.

The showcase, as such, is not limited to the arts market. Many industrial expos have product demonstrations of one form or another. There they fulfil a similar show-and-tell function. But in the arts the truncated showing has been increasingly problematic. Whereas a skilled commercial exhibitor can probably reveal the salient features of their piece of machinery or software in fifteen minutes, to provide an adequate realisation of a performance with just a slice of the show in that time is more challenging. One could argue that fifteen minutes of music can give the informed listener a good sense of skill, quality and appeal. Likewise, with dance. In the case of a theatre production, particularly one reliant on the spoken word, a fifteen-minute excerpt might tell its audience little. How much would we glean of *King Lear* if the mock trial on the blasted heath was all we were invited to see?

So the question of how to showcase has vexed market organisers from day one. Co-locating a market with a festival has been one partial solution. That was APAM's way for many years. Alignment with the National Festival of Australian Theatre in Canberra, and later the Adelaide Festival/Adelaide Fringe, enabled APAM to include some of their program, or access to it by delegates, on a favoured-nation basis. This method existed alongside the short-excerpt showcase selected and presented by the market in-house. By the time of the Brisbane markets, full-length showcases had been added.

By contrast, CINARS in the absence of a parallel festival created an 'on' and 'off' showcase program which also left a mix of short and full-length work. So in either case, any number of artists could choose to just find a space to self-present and hope to drum up enough attendances by ambush marketing to make it worthwhile. It is hit and miss but, as happens with the sale of a house, sometimes just one buyer will do.

Showcases relate to finished product or what is known as 'tour-ready'. There are also works in prospect; concepts and plans for a show; and it is here that the 'pitches' come into play. They are ten minutes of fame in which the artists and/or their producer stand up and spruik their idea. They seek commissioning or co-producing partners; and, further along, presenting opportunities. Sometimes they act simply as a heads-up. No doubt they were derived from the Broadway backers' showing, in which a rough draft of a prospective Broadway show is given a Sunday morning outing in a chilly Manhattan venue before prospective investors. The pitch is now pretty much a fixture in all arts markets, though there is little hard evidence of outcomes. Goodwill and interest of a 'let's see what happens' kind may be expressed.

Rarely has anyone, anywhere, instantly put money on the table. However, as an exercise in spreading the word, the pitch has value as a gamble. An instant response and as stark.

Another now-almost-universal practice is that of 'speed dating' at markets. Arguably one of the more grotesque notions ever introduced to the cultural domain, this consists of the producers sitting at tables with their video and other wares while presenters scurry around the room at fifteen-minute intervals to get the goods on dozens of shows related in a terrifying fast-forward manner. This intrepid delegate recently attended a market in Mexico in which he did twelve such meetings in three hours each morning for three days: 36 speeded dates. The alternative is for the presenters to sit still while the producers scurry. What value do these encounters engender?

Since a function of the market is to lure and hopefully induct new attendees, or victims if you prefer, many have invented welcoming devices. There are a myriad of 'buddy' systems for new members: veterans are assigned to look after new members, introduce them to other players and offer them the low communion of their cult. Markets can be bewildering experiences and like going to a cocktail party on one's own, a friend's arm is always helpful. Some of these mechanisms are more elaborate: first timers' morning teas, drinks or lunches—even advice on what to do and how to do it—and advance webinar information sessions. Why not? Markets are lions' dens and tyros need all the help they can get.

6. The rise of the Machines

Gatekeepers

As hinted earlier, beyond those overt trading posts festivals, fringe festivals and their equivalent also operate as marketplaces. It could be argued that many do so more effectively than the markets themselves. Even allowing for the pleasure and sometimes profit they derive, does anyone not see the Edinburgh or Adelaide Fringe as a market?

There is another factor. The proliferation of markets has created another layer of gatekeepers to the arts. They have elevated the role of the artist manager/agent as negotiators and brokers in the relationship between producers and presenters, sellers and buyers. They have reinforced the role of the presenter as custodian of the faith; but with the agent/broker/go-between as a sort of missionary of that cult, possessing rituals and special language to offer the baptism of being programmed somewhere, sometime. This has had consequences in the way the wider marketplace operates. More than anything, it has led to group action by presenters such as the US booking consortia and their parallels elsewhere. A circling of the wagon that further enhances the gatekeeper role.

The Festival phenomenon

But let us consider the equally gatekeeping festival phenomenon. From the 1970s onwards it seemed as though, in Europe at least, a festival of something materialised on every street corner. Artists and producers swarmed and with them came a new generation of go-betweens: booking, deal-making, shaping and reshaping the scene. Artists benefitted, some hugely. The panorama of European summer festivals gave a platform for practitioners of all art forms including those that were then freshly born, like the 'new' circus or physical theatre. Some, whose reputations survive and even thrive to this day, found their first showcase there. Many more fell by the wayside.

We have also seen the 'festivalising' of arts centres where clumps of programming have evolved, sometimes by theme: youth, Indigenous; by genre: dance, guitar, cabaret; by time of year: 'summerfare' or the equinoctial *Fête de la Musique* and sometimes both, e.g. Spring Dance and Fall for Dance and their ilk. All these deliver presenting modes into the hands of a perceived élite who increasingly control the scene and sadly are not always as skilled or knowledgeable in their craft as we might desire. Amid all this, like roaring lions, the buyers prowl the aisles seeking what sensational arts product they might devour.[47]

The Fringe

If we take Edinburgh to be the working model of the large multi-arts festival, its creation in 1947 set a trend that has covered the globe ever since. Then came the Fringe. As the name implies, the first Fringes were spawned beside a major festival, sometimes as a response to its perceived élitism. Again, Edinburgh provides the template and its Fringe is still the most visited. Reputations have been made and dashed there. It is the happy hunting ground of presenters looking for something startling, raunchy or cutting edge. Its success has led to a rash of imitators sitting alongside their older, often more staid and costly, mainline festival cousins. Avignon and Adelaide are prime examples of enormous thriving Fringes. They became platforms for aspiring, off-the-wall acts of every genre. The Fringe audience was mostly young, attracted by cheap tickets, the 'off main street' feel, the club-like atmosphere and perhaps above all the gladiatorial prospect of thumbs up or down. You paid your money and you took your chance and word of mouth was king.

Emerging artists brought their usually minimalist shows, put them on for a split-of-the-door in pubs, shopfronts, busted cinemas, chilly courtyards or stifling tents, packed the house or played to their mothers and moved on. Up the road in the 'real' Festivals, high art was taking place: *Hamlet* in Lithuanian, the Ulan Bator Philharmonic or the latest dance co-production between Paris and the Seychelles for $195 a seat. From the moment when eight student groups turned up in Edinburgh uninvited in 1947, the Fringe was a reaction against all that. But deep down every artist knew that if they got noticed at the Fringe, maybe next year in someone's mainstream festival somewhere else, audiences would be paying top dollar to see them.

For a while at least, those open-ended practices stymied the big festival gatekeepers. Here was self-selection as a business model and from its Edinburgh origins it spread like wildfire. Reputations—and from that careers—were and are made. Today, not all Fringes are wide open. Some are curated to a degree, often so as to give the producer and artists the chance of a break-even. Now 'off' and 'off off' even 'off off off' programs sit side by side with the core festival; and are subject to varying degrees and processes of selection or auto-selection. Threading through these mazes is an art in itself. Yet, whatever the methodology, they all function as markets. Everyone is here to be bought or sold whether direct by the public or more crucially by the roving packs of presenters and agents from elsewhere.

Other gatekeepers

Nevertheless, for a while rampant democracy prevailed and in some places still does. Gradually, producers and promoters found a way through this self-determination. 'Gardens' and Speigeltents and the Assembly Rooms, offered venues, umbrella marketing, strength in numbers and a variety of deals in exchange for heightened visibility, a more secure economic prospect but also the loss of freedom to decide one's own destiny. Some mechanisms have also risen to take advantage of all that. For instance, the Adelaide Fringe's 'Honey Pot' scheme seeks to make sense of the plethora of offerings there for international visitors by curating discrete, useful packages for them. The internet has been another means of side-stepping all kinds of gatekeepers. Artists, especially in those genres where live appearance is not critical, can achieve a million followers with one YouTube clip or a Facebook post. Careers have taken off from little else but that and raw talent.

7. Meeting new needs and new challenges

But what does all that now mean and what is it likely to mean in the future?

Maintaining Contact

Whatever view is taken of the market and whatever format is adopted, it is clear that the performing arts sector anywhere in the world generally lacks the means to keep the conversations started at one event going satisfactorily until the next. In North America and Europe, an abundance of artists' agents/managers fulfils that task to some extent. Australia generally lacks those conduits and the skills and experience, not to say perseverance, that go with them.

A small, but steadily growing number of Australian performing arts companies now have reliable international representation. Some have staff dedicated to keeping their work in front of the global community. They travel to other markets, visit presenters and advance conversation. For the most part, theirs are the productions that secure the lion's share of the dates. There is also a small number of Australian independent producers who represent companies or works on an international level, but fewer as time goes by. Notwithstanding some spectacular successes, all those discussed here are exceptions rather than the rule. In the Northern Hemisphere they are the rule.

Government arts agencies, notably but not exclusively the Australia Council, have tried to devise programs that will develop the skills needed for this work. However, the paucity of truly experienced mentors has limited their effectiveness. In the end, nothing beats first-hand knowledge and face-to-face experience. It is also noteworthy that with all of this, the most commonly expressed need across the sector is for training that focuses on the basics: negotiation, budgeting and promotion.

All this points to an acute lack of resources in Australia to underpin the export effort and through that the effectiveness of something like APAM. Even where an attempt has been made to offer resources, they are not always well deployed. For instance, though well intentioned, the OzArts scheme and later National Touring Selector were simply too reliant on busy companies and artists having to update their own entries. Most commercial experience shows that self-input sites rarely meet their objectives. With the best will, it is this writer's view that APAM's attempt to float this idea again will likely meet a similar fate.

A digital world

Some years ago I observed in a scoping study on future options for APAM:

> *By contrast, the targeted use of social networking might generate benefits. Programs of advice and market sensitivity might be maintained between conferences through monitored blogs. But these would have to be managed proactively and would need to ensure the regular involvement of key participants. They could not be left to be self-generating. Such sites might be useful places for good news stories and experiences about touring to be run. All that implies a more continuous and proactive management system than APAM currently has in place. Delivering that may prove to be the most critical change that could be made to APAM and the service it 'offers'.[48]*

It would be interesting to see if that or something like it can in fact be achieved.

When APAM was created in the mid-1990s most of the communication technologies and emergent e-commerce and social networking platforms that we now take for granted were in their infancy. FAX was cutting edge. No-one had a web page. In order to be seen, we had to be present. Today, anyone, anywhere in the world at any time can now see the newest show on YouTube. We can have an hour-long webcam conversation from Adelaide to Amsterdam for no cost. Some people even rehearse this way.

That is not to say that these means have replaced seeing a work or meeting the artist in person. In all probability, they never will. But they have revolutionised *access* to knowledge of the work and are creating and maintaining contact about it. In addition, as platforms for creativity as well as communication, these new media have shaped and reshaped our awareness of the way we interact, work and do business around the world. That, in turn, has led to an upsurge in creative collaborations and co-productions among artists separated by distance and time zones. There has also been a prodigious increase in competition with tens of thousands of artists and companies worldwide striving for the attention of a few hundred key presenters. Needless to add, technology has also refashioned habits of public consumption.

Meanwhile, there is another elephant in the room: the entire face-to-face market model is based on continued extensive international air travel, not only to assemble delegates at one or more market-like events in Australia—a great distance by anyone's standards—but to continue to support international touring itself. Despite Qantas's optimistic claims of being carbon neutral by 2050, there is already a known, marked reluctance among those concerned at the threat of climate change to use such transport. Artists are at the forefront of those concerns. Where then does that leave this whole house of cards? And where is the APAM risk assessment of that?

All those developments have changed the landscape within which we operate as purveyors of arts production, and the ways in which we strive to inform and influence others about our work. So the question is: how special does APAM need to be as a market to stand out in that increasingly crowded and noisy world? The answer would seem to be: much more special than it is.

All this suggests that there is a case for thinking about how emerging arts practice, the application of technology and our place in the region, might shape a future APAM and, within that, how to weigh 'exchange' against 'market' as its core purpose.

Who is it for?

On the one hand, the arts market model is tried and true. On the other, if any market mechanism is to continue to be distinctive and ultimately relevant, it will need to cast off some of the thinking that has shaped it over the past sixty years. Take our Australian event: why does it seem to focus on the not-for-profit sector to the exclusion of others?

It is a curiosity of the performing arts in Australia that many of its operatives act as though there was a wall dividing the for-profit from the not-for-profit. Yet even casual examination of the way work is generated indicates that to be a misreading. The performing arts are predicated on artists of many practices who move easily across such lines of demarcation. Equally, presenters, whether regional or global, do not distinguish, but book what works for them.

Of course, it could be argued that nothing prevents anyone from registering as a delegate to any market. Presumably, too, only lack of space would prevent anyone from hiring a booth and promoting their wares in the exhibition hall. In fact, a few 'commercial' or quasi-commercial producers have attended APAM over the years. Yet, if a producer who wore the badge of 'commercial' attempted to gain a showcase spot there, it is improbable that they would succeed. By contrast, PAX/PAC has no such problem. That is perhaps because, being a membership-based organisation, it knows that its presenting constituents want a spectrum of work for their consideration, not just an arbitrarily classified one.

Accordingly, I wonder why APAM has come to be about just one part of the industry and not about the whole. That seems peculiarly counterproductive given the Asian presenters who are touted as being among Australia's prime targets. The report covering the period 2014–2018 of the Brisbane-based APAM events[49] noted the relatively small contingent of Asian delegates in the first year; and how, despite significant further effort, more attendees but relatively little genuine market growth was achieved over the six-year period. Yet there seems little interest in the view that perhaps we choose to show our Asian delegates not what they might *want* to see but instead persist in showcasing what we think they *ought* to see. Australia's for-profit producers generally have more experience and success in Asia than our non-profits. Why would we not want to draw on that? Given the size of the Australian industry and its domestic capacity, can we afford not to maximise the benefits aimed at the general good?

Small to Medium

Among other constricting factors on the field in Australia was the decision that APAM should focus on the lugubriously termed 'small-to-medium sector'. This condescending expression, like most adopted by bureaucracy, has never been adequately explained. Is it scale of operation? Is a one person performance small in this sense? Is Meow Meow small? Or Robyn Archer? Is it suggested that the practice is miniature, the ideas are small? Or that being not large is somehow a weakness in need of The Showcase help?

But how is the focus on this small-to-medium sector to the exclusion of others justified? The argument, if it is advanced, that the large and powerful can help themselves, is unproven. It would certainly come as a surprise to IMG and CAMI who show no reluctance to promote their wares at APAP and anywhere buyers congregate. Imagine if chambers of commerce excluded Australia's largest employers and most visible contributors to their industries on the grounds that only small business should be supported.

Music, too, has been all but excluded from APAM (rarely above eight per cent of content)—to the market's detriment. That was another arbitrary decision made with little consultation, and to the dismay of music producers. Many felt they were even further excluded from the 'small to medium sector' despite being so obviously a part of it. Some music genres have meanwhile had to find other ways of promoting themselves, both within Australia and notably through the periodic Sounds Australian showcases in North America and elsewhere abroad.

The Maturing of the Sector

Along with what now seem like primitive selling tools, when the Australian performing arts sector set out on the market journey, it had relatively few international scores on the board. Most regular international touring was in music, and few larger producers had made a mark. A handful of small, largely self-promoted companies had made inroads into specialist markets and once-off productions or individual artists achieved overseas tour bookings through a combination of chance and chutzpah. Australian government promotions and the efforts of diplomatic posts accounted for other exposure. Yet it was, for the most part, hit and miss.

The establishment of APAM offered a focus for what had been disparate. Crucially, it raised the bar and brought Australian producers and artists face-to-face with overseas presenters in an intensive encounter. Moreover, it forced them to think about what they did, why they did it and how they presented it for consideration. Some succeeded, others failed. It compelled some to acknowledge that however significant their work might appear locally, internationally it might not fly. Moreover, it engendered the notion that this was about *selling* work, not *giving it away*. But whatever the history and whatever the processes, for most of its life APAM remained essentially transactional in its assumptions.

To suggest that this maturing occurred quickly would be naïve. It's probable that to this day most Australian performing arts companies aspiring to overseas touring lack the skill, the critical tools or the preparedness to make this happen, irrespective of the quality of their product. But over time, there have been companies that have learned on the job, made connections and blazed some trails. Few now expect instant gratification in sales and most recognise that all relationships take time to mature and show benefits. Today, there is a danger that all that may be at risk of being dismantled.

The Region

At the same time, another question arises. Should whatever Australian mechanism is employed be about the region, rather than just Australia? Should it be genuinely an international showcase rather than one that pushes only the national barrow? Over time, many have expressed concern about the absence of cultural diversity in APAM beyond the inclusion of First Nations work, which has only relatively recently come to occupy a central place. All worry about the face of Australia that APAM has presented to the region. The linkage with AsiaTopa may serve to change that under the new rubric, but it still looks dismayingly like the promotion of an Australo-Asian enclave rather than the opening of a major door. Reciprocity may be a better solution.

Again, CINARS probably comes closest to offering a model and a method. Early in its history its management recognised that there was not enough work of quality in Quebec or even in Canada to keep delegates coming back. Accordingly, it opened its showcase to all comers. Productions from elsewhere are still a minority, but there is no 'national' barrier to application. That also applies to other foreign markets where anyone offshore can apply to showcase but only a few will be chosen. In fact, most overseas companies edit themselves out because of the expense. Sometimes 'focus' nations at a market support their artists to make a special showing. Equally, anyone who can make the cut could in theory showcase in any of the US markets. Yet few do, other than at APAP, and there usually off-site. There is no reason to suppose that the result would be any different were APAM to follow. However, the gain in profile and in diversity of program and attendance could be considerable. Should there be concerns about the danger of imbalance with too much 'foreign' product, it would always be possible to impose a cap.

Many pathways

However, APAM has never been the only way to pursue the export goal. Nor has it ever been the sole instrument. In the 25 years of its existence the Australian Government has trialled and continues to trial other strategies. These have included: Australia Council support of Australian artists and producers to attend markets and comparable events in other countries; in-bound visitor programs to key festivals and other major viewing sites either individually or in groups; the support of key advocates off-shore in Europe, North America, East Asia and South-east Asia; and a range of brokering activities in other regions begun at various times though often abruptly and inexplicably abandoned.

The Department of Foreign Affairs and Trade, likewise, has long had in-bound cultural visitor programs which have paralleled or intersected some of the Australia Council's initiatives. Some posts, as well as the bilateral bodies such as the Australia China Council and Australia Indonesia Institute, have been active over many decades in support of artistic residencies and exchanges.

So, depending on your point of view, Australian artists have had the benefit of many pathways to international exposure, or the disincentive of having to thread their way through a thicket of programs and mechanisms to find their place in the international sun. Some few, inevitably, choose to make their own way regardless, and a scattering succeed. In that respect, they are no different from those in other industries who choose to eschew government export programs and find their own markets for their product. Of course, for any artistic product there are also many starting and finishing points. Different companies pursue different strategies and, for that reason, generalising about 'best practice' is not always helpful.

I will use one example here. It is close to my heart and I make no apology for that. For nearly 25 years I have been associated with Marrugeku, an intercultural dance company which is based in Broome but travels the world.[50] Their work often emerges from an international intercultural choreographic laboratory held periodically. Four years ago they conducted one such in Noumea with dancers of Aboriginal and settler background, New Caledonians of Kanak and Asian heritage and mentors from West Papua, Australia and Burkina Faso. However, holding the lab in that location was the outcome of a twenty-year practice of taking previous productions to Noumea and each time deepening and widening cultural and (as it happened) political conversation. Out of that lab came a new work, *Le Dernier Appel*, which was successively pitched at APAM and PAX and promoted at CINARS. It was ultimately co-commissioned by Carriageworks in Sydney, Arts House in Melbourne, *Centre Culturel Tjibaou* in Noumea and *Théâtre National Chaillot* in Paris. It premiered in Sydney and Noumea, toured to Adelaide and Melbourne as well as Belgium and France.

Now comes the market conundrum of which my title speaks: all of those stages were factors in the export journey. It would be hard to say which encounter was more influential than another but importantly all relied on relationships that had begun well before even that initial lab and before any of us turned up at a market. Looking back, I ask myself: would I forego any one of the stages? No. Could I, after forty years of export experience, have accurately predicted the way forward? No. Would I use that journey to argue for the benefit of arts markets? Like Zhou Enlai's famous reply on the significance of the French Revolution: 'Too soon to tell.'

8. Maybe a way forward

So, where does this leave us? Weighing the options and taking into account all its curious and at times frustrating aspects, on balance I am inclined to believe that the more or less conventionally designed performing arts market still has a role to play in the way in which we seek to trade the performing arts nationally and internationally.

Certainly, I don't think any of it in Australia has been a waste of public or of artists' money. We can all think of too many Australian companies that have been advantaged. But despite the reports I've quoted here, the cost-benefit analysis is always somewhat opaque and, frankly, there have been smoke and mirrors involved from time to time.

That said, even in the face of the many changes and adaptations to the primary model, and growth in numbers, there is little evidence that delegates are obtaining greater satisfaction or that critically, the markets themselves are more effective in their core business of buying and selling than they once were. It may be argued that the transactional dimension of the market/meeting/exchange is a thing of the past and that the networking, by whatever term, is or should be what it is really all about. Perhaps there is truth in that. But any conference might achieve networking. Deep down, my hunch is that, in one way or another, delegates still come to the market to trade or learn how to trade.

However, there are impediments to continuing on the same path. Every day the world becomes more crowded with arts product on offer. Presenters are overwhelmed. No-one, anywhere, has found more effective means to deal with this oversupply. It is likely that, for the foreseeable future, the face-to-face encounter will continue to be the best way. However, that is already under challenge by the proponents of the carbon neutral world and unless we revert to helium-powered airships, it is hard to see that abating.

Equally, while much of the market mechanism is now driven by digital representation and sales material, the performing arts world has hardly scratched the surface of the possibilities of VR and AR as ways for producers to bring their product to the attention of presenters. Whatever the new APAM model brings, it must give more attention to that dimension or we shall truly be left behind. In other industries digital highways are being utilised to develop conversation in advance of a market event so as to help shape it. Small coteries either in quasi-state agencies or appointed by them, still function as the overly influential gatekeepers to showcasing content, who get to pitch what and how encounters are framed. We have the tools to involve as many of the potential delegates as we might wish, so that before and during and after there could be real and advanced judgement, real input and real outcomes—and, dare I say it, real democracy. Despite the reforms, APAM is still somebody else's market. It is not and never has been the practitioners' market. That too must change.

In the absence of those relatively simple steps, we continue mystifyingly to trudge along a path so little different from that of the market's inventors sixty years ago. Despite the bells and whistles it is still a very big crowd in a large space, in an arts centre or hotel conference room, trying to work out why they are there, what they can get out of the experience, who they will meet or have failed to meet, and whether in the end it was all worthwhile.

Every arts market in the world endeavours to track response. How many of those who have been funded by their employer to attend, especially if that happens to be a local government authority, are going to say: 'No, it was a complete waste of time' and 'I would never go again!' That is not how the world turns.

Speaking of the very big crowd, we should not overlook the fact that the sheer assembling periodically of a large number of colleagues in one place has a value of its own. Certainly, if we consider the over 600 delegates, overwhelmingly from Australia and New Zealand, who attend APAM every two years, togetherness is a large driver. Australia, like the United States and Canada, is an immense land mass with scattered population. Unlike Europe, you cannot get on the train and be in another country in 90 minutes. Therefore, such gatherings have value beyond the trading mechanism.

One of the dangers posed by the new APAM model in subdividing itself over a number of the pre-existing festival-type activities, is that it will lose that critical mass. As it is, holding a number of events in one year as opposed to one large gathering every two years, is already likely to present problems of over-frequency and therefore reduced, proportionate attendance. The focus at AsiaTopa on Australian/Asian work, on the one hand, and on First Nations work at the Darwin Festival on the other, runs the risk of reducing the range of interest among international delegates or even national delegates whose obligation is to present in their venues a wide spectrum. The cost and time factor of coming to Australia every two years was already a major obstacle for many, even when it was still a market that laid out a smorgasbord of productions. It seems likely that the subdivision proposed in the new model might severely dilute this offering. Only time will tell.

The direction APAM is taking also adds to, and may well exacerbate, the competition that has already occurred through the creation of the biennial Dance Massive in Melbourne and to some extent the annual Live Works in Sydney. Not to mention the many Fringes. Each has attracted international attention but in specialised ways. If that fracturing continues, I wonder how any critical mass will be sustained. Accordingly, I fear the decision to dissipate the big picture in favour of many smaller ones will prove a mistake. I hope I am wrong.

While the dismantling of the old APAM scheme

has been taking place, as we have seen the annual PAX market and its umbrella organisation PAC grow. As a market PAX still lacks an international dimension and some degree of sophistication, though both seem to be increasing. In late 2019 they announced that the two would merge into APAX—the Australian Performing Arts Exchange, stating that: '98 per cent of people coming to PAX and the conferences this year said that "Market and audience development are a critical part of the performing arts sector".'[51] They may in time challenge APAM for its place as the major performing arts gathering for the nation and New Zealand. Again, only time will tell.

In closing, I return to the theme implied in this essay: people do business with those they know and the better they know them the more likely it is that they will do business over and again. Regular opportunities for meeting and talking and learning are a central factor in maintaining such relationships—call them friendships if you will—and to the extent that such meeting and talking can be structured, goodwill and trust is gained and grown over time and when all is said and done, no amount of technology or wizardry of other kinds has yet found a better way.

Endnotes

All digital references accessed by the author were valid at time of printing.

1   https://apap365.org
2   https://cinars.rg
3   https://apam.org.au
4   Spate, O.H.K, *The Spanish Lake*. Canberra: ANU Press, 1979, p.13.
5   https://www.tpam.or.jp
6   Media Release, 'Sydney Festival 2020', 30 October 2019.
7   Sandra Gattenhof, with Georgia Saffrin and Michelle Grant, 'The Evaluation of the Australian Performing Arts Market 2014 to 2018—Three Year Executive Summary' QUT, 2018.
8   https://paca.org.au
9   Angus & Robertson, 1976.
10 http://www.pannz.org.nz
11 'Australian Performing Arts Market, 22 to 26 February 2010.' Adelaide Festival Centre, Final Report', Arts Projects Australia, June 2010.
12 https://capacoa.ca
13 https://www.ispa.org
14 https://www.artsnw.org
15 https://www.westarts.org

16   https://pae.southarts.org

17   https://www.artsmidwest.org

18   https://ipayweb.org

19   Andrew Bleby, 'Australian Performing Arts Market 1994—2002', Bleby Arts Management, May 2003 p.4.

20   cf Gattenhof, especially 'Impact Stories from CASE Study Companies and Independent Artists' pp.25 ff.

21   Bleby, p.7.

22   Gattenhof.

23   APAM 2018 Final Report.

24   APAM 'Final Reports': 2014, 2016 and 2018.

25   Macdonnell, Justin. 'Australian Performing Arts Market Scoping Study, Anzarts Institute Limited, February 2011.

26   APAM 'Program Overview', June 2019..

27   http://www.showcasewa.com.au.

28   https://showcasesa.com.au

29   https://artsontour.com.au/aot-salon

30   http://www.artour.com. au

31   https://www.showcasevictoria.com.au

32   cf 'Australian Arts Markets Survey', PAC updated May 2018.

33   https://www.creativenz.govt.nz

34   http://www.capa.com.cn

35   https://en.pams.or.kr

36   https://adam.tpac-taipei.org

37   https://www.bipam.org

38   https://www.en.masa.ci

39 https://doadoa.org
40 http://www.sibfest.ro/bursa
41 https://dublintheatrefestival.ie/programme/festival-plus/26th-international-theatre-exchange-itx
42 http://mapasmercadocultural.com/es
43 https://fonca.cultura.gob.mx/enartes
44 https://www.festivaldeteatro.com.co/via
45 Sergio Ramirez, musician, academic and cultural manager, conversation with the Author, Guadalajara May 2019.
46 BBC, 1996.
47 With apologies to 1: Peter 5:8
48 Macdonnell.
49 Gattenhof.
50 https://www.marrugeku.com
51 Rick Heath, 'The Future of PAX and PAC—Australia's Performing Arts Conference', 19 December 2019.

COPYRIGHT
INFORMATION

PLATFORM PAPERS
Quarterly essays from Currency House Inc.
Founding Editor: Dr John Golder
Editor: Katharine Brisbane
Currency House Inc. is a non-profit association and resource centre
advocating the role of the performing arts in public life by research,
debate and publication.
Postal address: PO Box 2270, Strawberry Hills, NSW 2012, Australia
Email: info@currencyhouse.org.au Tel: (02) 9319 4953
Website: www.currencyhouse.org.au Fax: (02) 9319 3649
Editorial Committee: Katharine Brisbane AM, Michael Campbell,
Dr Julian Meyrick, Martin Portus, Dr Nick Shimmin,
Dr Liza-Mare Syron.

ISBN 978 0 6484265 5 4
ISSN 1449-583X
Typeset in Garamond
Production by Currency Press Pty Ltd
Printed by Fineline Print + Copy Services, Revesby, NSW.